No, you're not.

Jimbo Matison's fault

ABRAMS BOOKS FOR YOUNG READERS
NEW YORK

The illustrations in this book were made with deliciously
fun brush and ink linework, happily colored in Photoshop.

Library of Congress Cataloging-in-Publication Data

Matison, Jimbo.
I'm going to catch my tail! / by Jimbo Matison.
pages cm
Summary: A rambunctious kitten wakes from
a nap determined to catch its tail.
ISBN 978-1-4197-1382-8
[1. Cats—Fiction. 2. Animals—Infancy—Fiction. 3. Humorous stories.]
I. Title. II. Title: I am going to catch my tail!
PZ7.M4293lm 2014
2013049747

Text and illustrations copyright © 2014 Jimbo Matison
Book design by Chad W. Beckerman
and Jimbo Matison

Printed and bound in China
10 9 8 7 6 5 4 3 2 1

Abrams Books for Young Readers are available at special
discounts when purchased in quantity for premiums and
promotions as well as fundraising or educational use. Special
editions can also be created to specification. For details,
contact specialsales@abramsbooks.com
or the address below.

THE ART OF BOOKS SINCE 1949
115 West 18th Street
New York, NY 10011
www.abramsbooks.com

For Irving, who is
happily sleeping now.

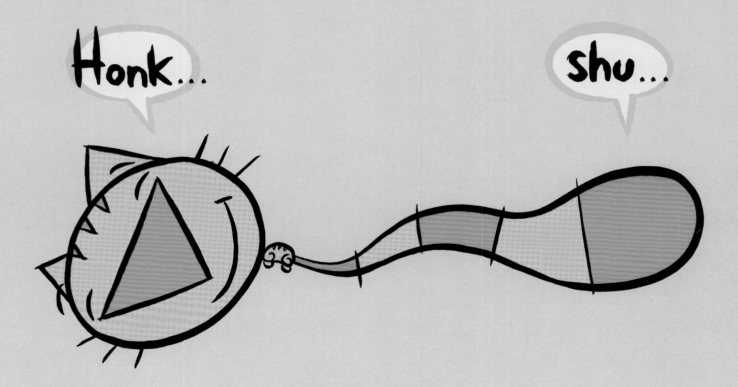

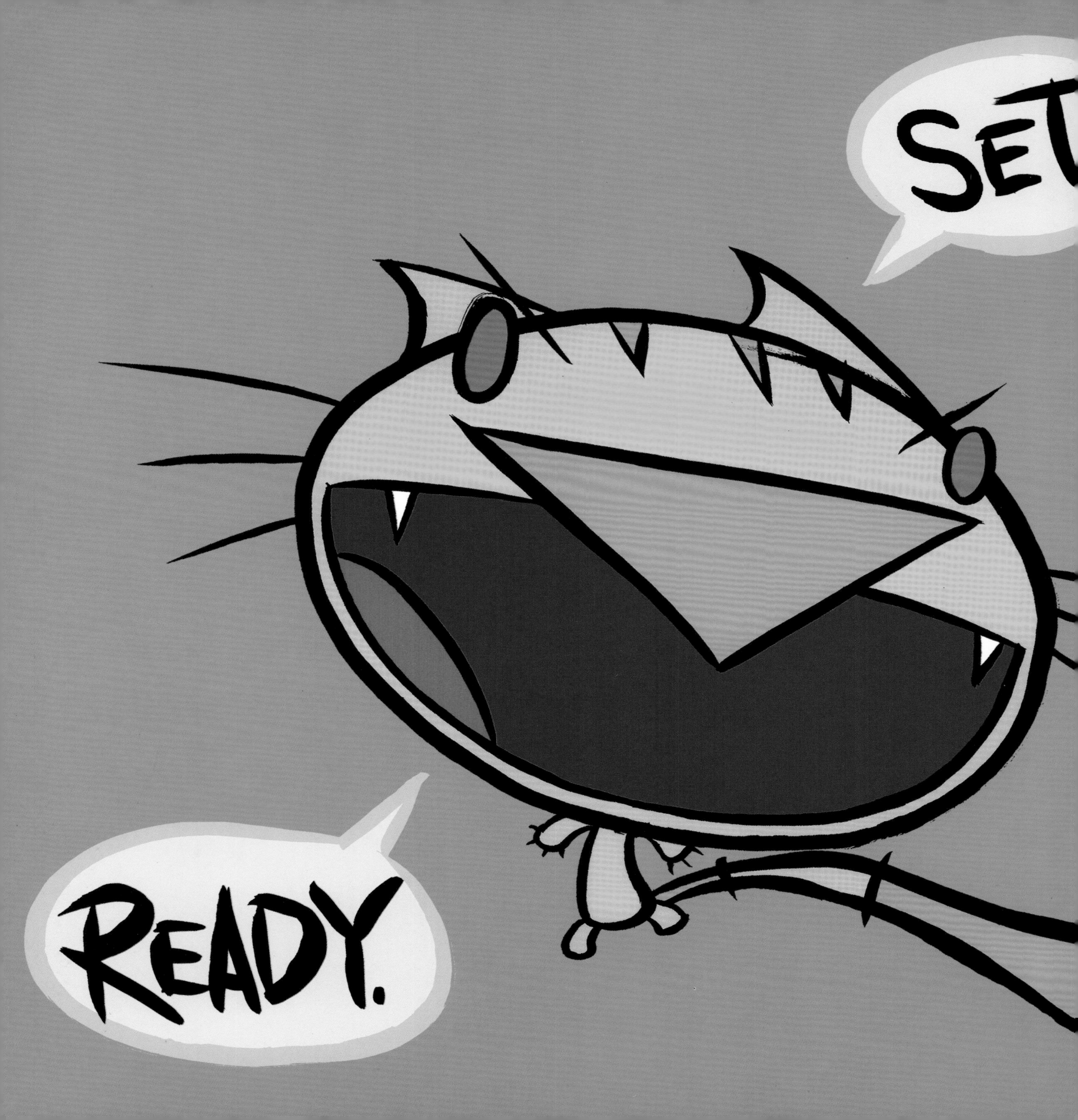
READY.
SET

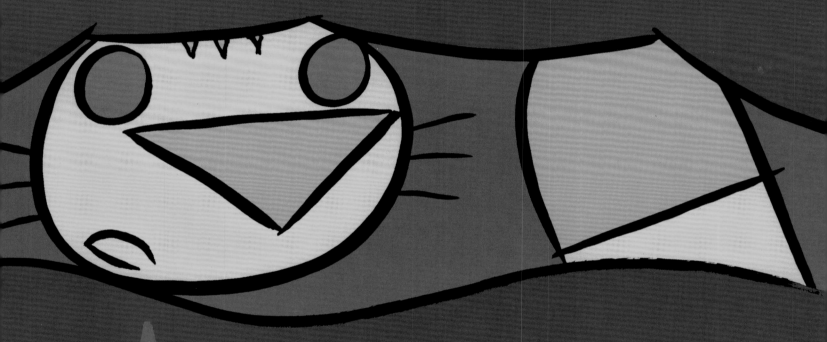

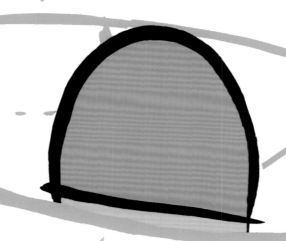

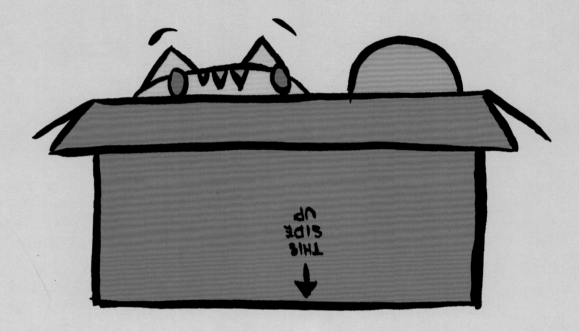

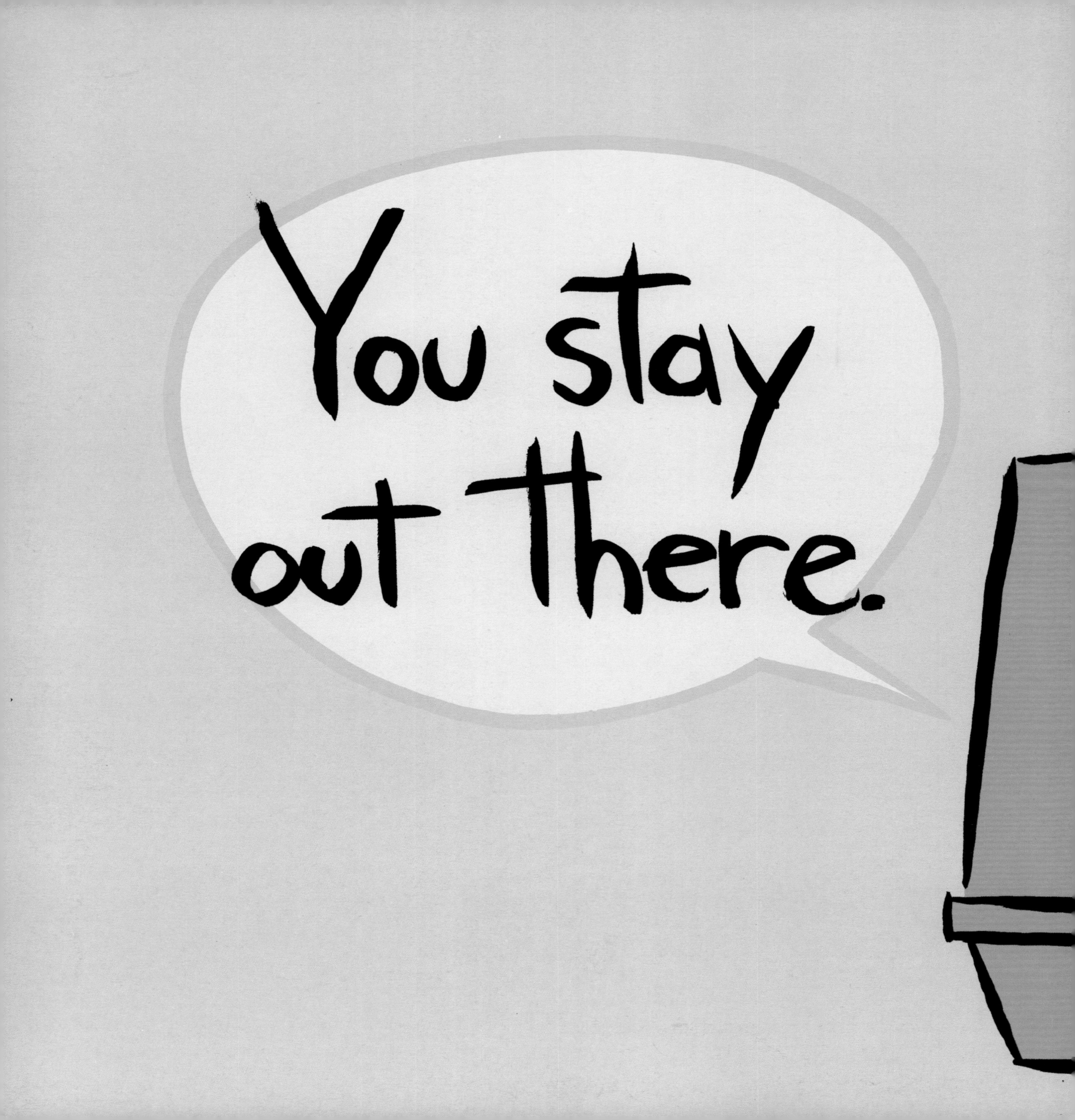
You stay out there.

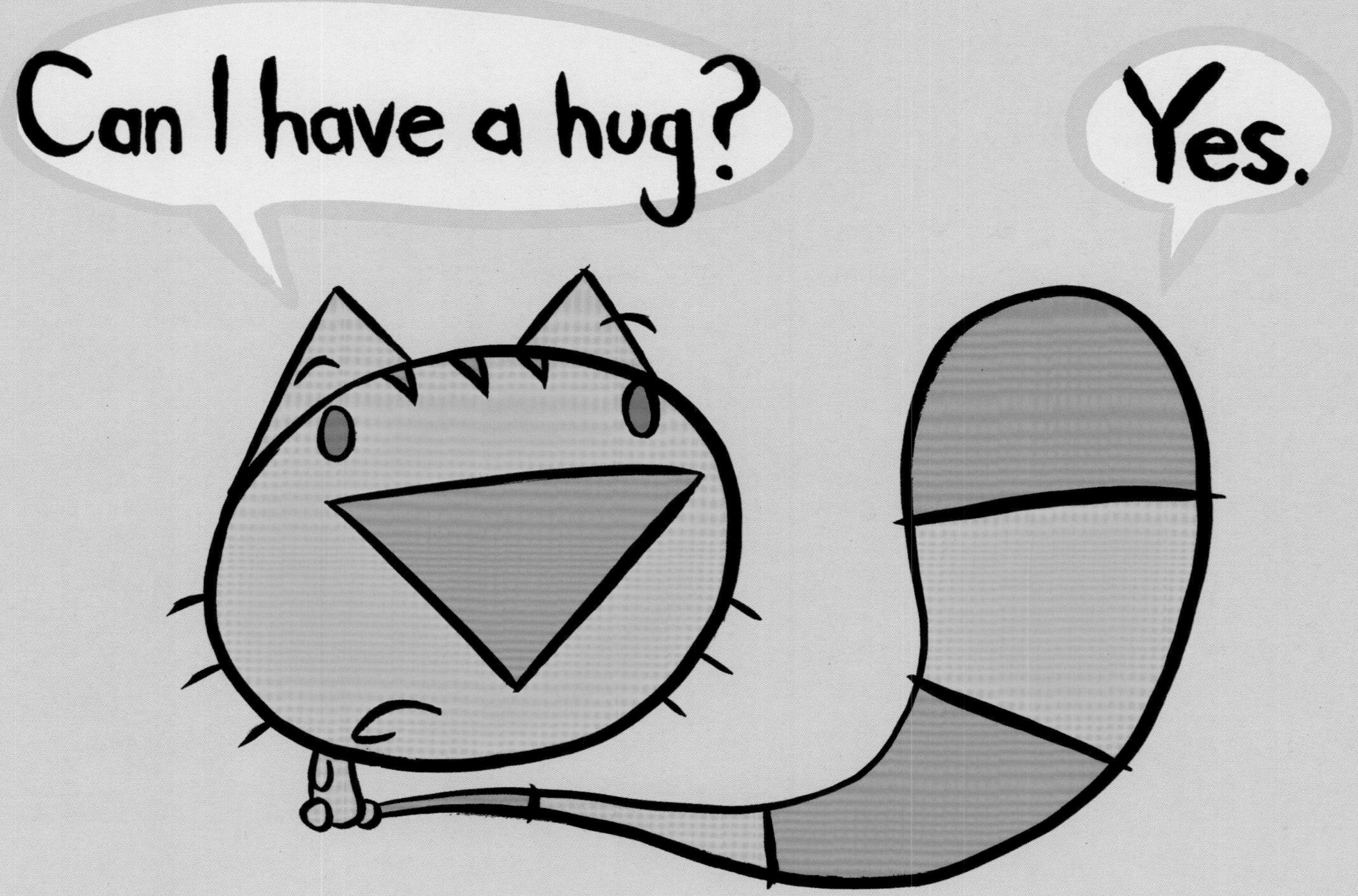
Can I have a hug?
Yes.

=Hug=